Sesame Street Start-to-Read Books™
help young children take a giant step into reading.
The stories have been skillfully written, designed,
and illustrated to provide funny, satisfying
reading experiences for the child just starting out.
Let Big Bird, Bert and Ernie, Oscar the Grouch,
and all the Sesame Street Muppets get your child
into reading early with these wonderful stories!

On Sesame Street,
Gordon is played by Roscoe Orman.

Copyright © 1988 Children's Television Workshop. Sesame Street MUPPETS © Muppets, Inc. 1988. All rights reserved under International and Pan-American Copyright Conventions. ® Sesame Street and Sesame Street sign are trademarks and service marks of the Children's Television Workshop. Published in the United States by Random House, Inc., New York, and simultaneously in Canada by Random House of Canada Limited, Toronto, in conjunction with the Children's Television Workshop.

Library of Congress Cataloging-in-Publication Data:
Hautzig, Deborah. It's a secret! (A Sesame Street start-to-read book) "Featuring Jim Henson's Sesame Street Muppets." SUMMARY: Bert is dismayed when Ernie tells the other Muppets his secret—that he cannot count over 100—but they soon make him feel better by teaching him to count that high. [1. Counting—Fiction.   2. Secrets— Fiction.   3. Puppets—Fiction]   I. Leigh, Tom, ill.   II. Title.   III. Series: Sesame Street start-to-read books. PZ7.H2888Is   1988   [E]   87-20542   ISBN: 0-394-89672-6 (trade); 0-394-99672-0 (lib. bdg.)
Manufactured in the United States of America   5 6 7 8 9 0

A Sesame Street Start-to-Read Book™

IT'S A SECRET!

by Deborah Hautzig • illustrated by Tom Leigh

Featuring Jim Henson's Sesame Street Muppets

Random House/Children's Television Workshop

Bert was looking for something.

He looked on the steps.

He looked on the sidewalk.

"What are you doing?"
growled Oscar the Grouch.

"Hunting for bottle caps!" said Bert.

"I have more bottle caps
than anyone!" Bert said.
"How many?" asked Oscar.
"More than 100," Bert said proudly.
"Oscar, do you have any for me?"

Oscar went to look.
Three bottle caps flew out
of his can.
"Thanks, Oscar!" said Bert.
"Now GO AWAY!" yelled Oscar.

Bert went down the street.

He looked in the flower box.

He looked under the mailbox.

He looked around the lamppost.

Big Bird came along and said,

"Are you looking for something?"

"Yes," said Bert.

"I will help you," said Big Bird.

Big Bird looked and looked.

"Say, Bert, what are we looking for?"

"Bottle caps!" said Bert.

Then Grover and Ernie came by.
"Hi! What are you doing?"
asked Ernie.
"We are busy bottle-cap hunting,"
said Bert.

"There are many bottle caps
in the park," said Grover.
"I, Grover the Finder,
will find them for you!"
So they all went to the park.

They found bottle caps everywhere.
Big Bird even found one in a tree!
"Birds like soda too," he said.

Soon they found 20.
They gave them all to Bert.
"Now how many bottle caps
do you have?" asked Grover.
"Oh, lots!" said Bert,
and he ran to the sandbox.

Ernie was digging in the sand
for bottle caps.
"Say, Bert, just how many
do you have?" asked Ernie.

"More than 100," said Bert.

"But how many more?" said Ernie.

Bert turned red.

Then he whispered in Ernie's ear,

"I don't know!"

"If I tell you a secret,
will you promise not to tell?"
asked Bert.

"Sure, Bert," said Ernie.
Bert looked around to make sure
nobody was listening.

"I can't count over 100!"
Ernie was amazed!

"REALLY?" shouted Ernie.

"You can't count—"

"Shhh!" said Bert. "It's a secret!"

"Don't worry," whispered Ernie.

"I won't tell."

On the way home they saw Betty Lou.
Next to her were
ten stacks of pennies.
"Hi, Betty Lou!" said Big Bird.
"What are you doing
with all those pennies?"

"I am trying to count them.
I want to buy a pretty scarf
for my mother's birthday,"
said Betty Lou. "The lady at the store
said I need 250 pennies.
But I cannot count up to 250!"

"Do not worry, Betty Lou,"
said Grover. "Bert will count them!"
"Sure, Bert can do it!"
said Big Bird.

"No he can't!" said Ernie.

Then he put his hand over his mouth.

"Oops," he said.

"Why not?" said Betty Lou.

"I can't tell," said Ernie.

"It's a secret."

"Oh, come on, Ernie!" said Big Bird.

"You can tell us.

We can keep a secret."

Bert glared at Ernie.

"Pretty please?" said Grover.

Ernie felt like
he was going to burst!
Finally he could not stand it.
"BERT CAN'T COUNT
OVER 100!"

"Ernie, how could you do that?
You told my secret!" cried Bert.
Two tears rolled down his face
and he ran away.

Ernie felt terrible!

"Oh, poor Bert!" said Grover.

"Gee, Bert should not feel bad,"
  said Big Bird. "I can't count past 20!"

"Oh, dear," said Ernie.

"I have to tell Bert
  that I am sorry."

Ernie found Bert
hiding under the sink.
"You told my secret," said Bert.
"I am sorry, old buddy," said Ernie.
"Why did you do that?" said Bert.
"I don't know," said Ernie.

"Now everyone thinks I am stupid,"
  said Bert.
"Oh, no, Bert! Everybody knows that
  you are very smart!
  I was stupid to tell.
  I am very sorry."
Bert smiled. "It's okay, Ernie.
  I understand."

Gordon knocked on the door.
Big Bird, Grover, and Betty Lou
came in with him.
"Please do not feel bad," said Grover.

Big Bird said, "I wrote a poem
to cheer you up, Bert.
"Oh, you can't count past 100,
It's true,
But no one makes oatmeal
As yummy as you!"

"Everybody has to learn to count,"
said Gordon.
"Bert, go get your bottle caps.
I will teach you how to count them."
Betty Lou shook her piggy bank.
Clink! Clink! went the pennies.
"Oh, will you teach me
how to count pennies?"
she asked.
"Yes," said Gordon.
"You count pennies the same way."

At sunset Bert and Betty Lou
finished counting.
"I have 368 bottle caps!"
said Bert proudly.
"I have 325 pennies,"
said Betty Lou happily.
"And I have two friends,"
said Gordon, "who are the best
counters on Sesame Street."

That night Bert counted the stars.
"501, 502, 503…"
counted Bert.
"I promise to be a better
secret keeper," said Ernie.
"Now can we please go to sleep?"